Awkward Aardvark

Other books Adrienne Kennaway:

Lazy Lion
Hot Hippo
Greedy Zebra
Hungry Hyena
Tricky Tortoise
Crafty Chameleon
Baby Baboon

A catalogue record for this book is available from the British Library.

ISBN 0 340 52581 9

Text copyright © Peter Upton 1989
Illustrations copyright © Adrienne Kennaway 1989

The right of Peter Upton and Adrienne Kennaway to be identified
as the author and illustrator of this Work has been asserted by them
in accordance with the Copyright, Designs and Patents Act 1988.

First published 1989
This edition published 2005

13 12 11 10 9

Hodder Children's Books
A division of Hodder Headline Limited
338 Euston Road, London NW1 3BH

Printed and bound in Hong Kong

Awkward Aardvark

By
Mwalimu

Illustrated by
Adrienne Kennaway

Hodder
Children's
Books

a division of Hodder Headline Limited

Aardvark was asleep in his favourite tree. The tree was old and dry, but it had a smooth branch where Aardvark would lie and rest his long nose.

And what a nose! His snoring was so loud that it kept Mongoose and all the other animals awake night after night. 'HHHRRR-ZZZZ!' went Aardvark's nose.

'How annoying,' Mongoose yawned. 'I wish he would keep quiet or go somewhere else.'

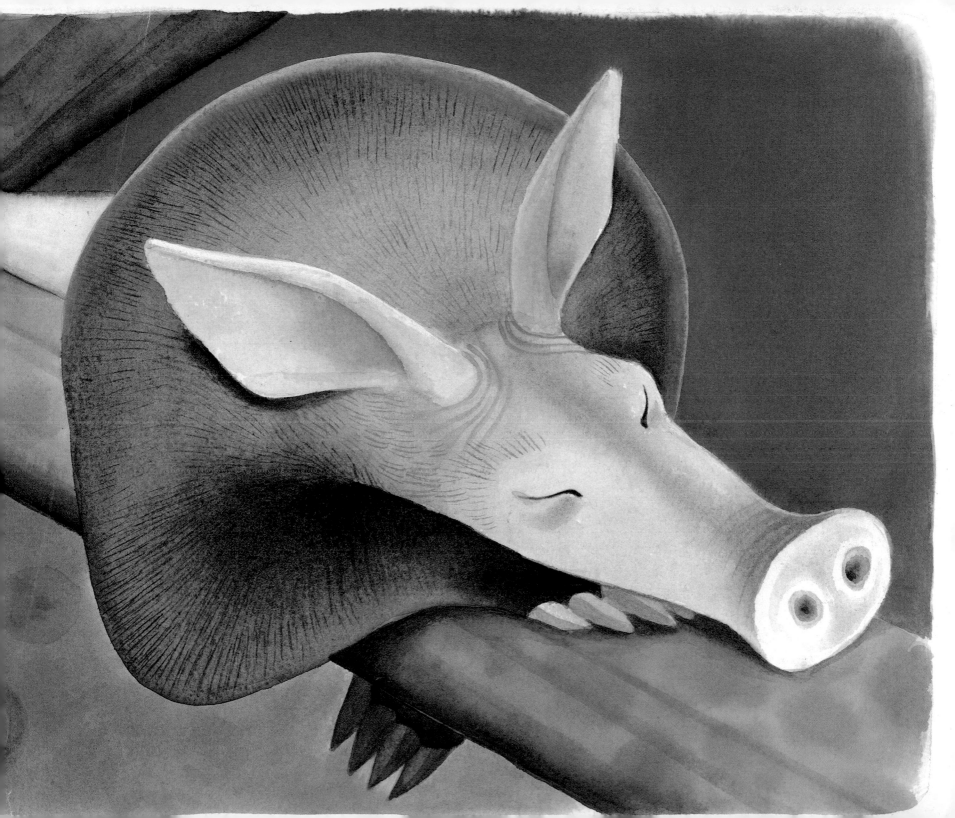

Aardvark only stopped
snoring when the sun came up.
Then he clambered to the ground
and set off to hunt for tasty grubs
and crunchy beetles.

While Aardvark was hunting
for breakfast, Mongoose
had an idea.
'I will just have to annoy
him more than he annoys
me,' he decided.

First Mongoose had a
meeting with the Monkeys.

Next he went to see Lion.

Then he talked to Rhinoceros.

That night, as usual, Aardvark climbed up to his branch in the tree and very soon he was snoring. 'HHHRRR-ZZZZ!'

Mongoose called into the darkness. The Monkeys came, and the tree shook as they chattered and screeched in the branches.

Aardvark woke up. 'Stop making that noise,' he shouted. But he soon went back to sleep and snored even more loudly than before. 'HHHRRR-ZZZZ!'

Then Mongoose
called out again. There
was a low, rumbling growl
as Lion came pad-pad-
padding to the tree where
Aardvark was snoring.

Stretching his legs and reaching high,
Lion SCRAAATCHED the bark with his strong claws.

Aardvark woke up again. 'Stop it! Go away!'
he shouted. But soon he was snoring again,
louder than ever. 'HHHRRR-ZZZZ!'

Now Mongoose was very angry. He was so angry that his fur bristled. He sent out another call. The ground trembled as Rhinoceros came puff-puff-puffing to the tree. BUMP! Aardvark nearly fell off the branch when Rhinoceros pushed his fat bottom against the trunk.

'Go away! Leave me alone!' cried Aardvark. But still he did not stay awake for long. 'HHHRRR-ZZZZ!'

'We need help,' puffed Rhinoceros. 'I'll tell you what we'll do.'

Soon there came a munch-munch-munching sound from the roots of the tree. Aardvark just kept on snoring.

Suddenly there was a loud snap and a crack. SNAP went the roots. CRAAAAACK went the tree and it toppled over.

Aardvark bounced to the ground.

He picked himself up and glared at the other animals.
'Who did that? Who pushed my tree over?' he demanded.

'Not me,' said Lion.
'Not me,' said Rhinoceros.
'Not us,' said the Monkeys.

Aardvark snorted at Mongoose.
'It was you.'
'Not me,' said Mongoose.
'They did it.' And he pointed
at the broken roots.

Aardvark saw that the roots of the tree had been eaten away by hundreds of termites.

'I'm going to gobble you up,' he threatened. He stuck out his long tongue and ate some of the termites. 'Yum-yum.' He licked his lips. 'I think I'll eat you all.'

The termites hurried away with Aardvark following and eating as many as he could reach with his tongue.

In the morning the termites hid in
the castles of sand and mud which
they had built to protect themselves.
But at night they still came out to
eat the trees.

And from that time to this,
Aardvark has slept during the day
and eaten termites at night.

And Mongoose and the other animals sleep
peacefully because they are no longer disturbed
by Awkward Aardvark's awful snoring.